Light Speed - Crossing Into the Void

Light Speed, Volume 3

Grayson Gray

Published by Grayson Gray, 2024.

This is a work of fiction. Similarities to real people, places, or events are entirely coincidental.

LIGHT SPEED -CROSSING INTO THE VOID

First edition. December 15, 2024.

Copyright © 2024 Grayson Gray.

ISBN: 979-8230912903

Written by Grayson Gray.

Also by Grayson Gray

Light Speed
Light Speed -Crossing Into the Void

Table of Contents

Light Speed - Crossing Into the Void
Light Speed-Volume 3
Grayson Gray
Published by Grayson Gray, 2024

LIGHT SPEED -CROSSING INTO THE VOID First edition. December 15, 2024. Copyright © 2024 Grayson Gray. Written by Grayson Gray

Prologue: -Editorial Universe Today.

The darkness stretched infinitely, a silent void swallowing all light, matter, and understanding. It was beyond human comprehension — a chasm in space-time born from a tragic event. Two ships, caught in an impossible collision, detonated their tachyon drives, opening a rift that rippled through the fabric of the universe. Where there had once been stars, dust, and cosmic bodies, now existed only the Rift — a shimmering mystery of twisted energies and impossible colors.

To those watching from a safe distance, the Rift was both beautiful and terrifying. It pulsed with energy, a kaleidoscope of greens, blues, and violets, cascading in waves and bursts, as if it were alive, breathing in the vacuum of space. Scientists back on Earth debate endlessly over the nature of this anomaly. Is it a tear in the fabric of reality? A window into another dimension? Or merely a distortion, a temporary fluctuation like the northern lights soon to fade away?

But the Rift shows no signs of fading. If anything, it seems to grow, its boundaries expanding, its energy intensifying. Telescopes and satellites have captured fleeting glimpses of strange, unidentifiable phenomena within its depths: shapes and shadows that seem to dance just beyond the limits of human sight.

In the midst of the chaos, one ship was chosen to make the first foray into the unknown. The ESS *Destiny*, a starship crewed by some of humanity's finest explorers, was given a single directive: investigate the Rift, uncover its secrets, and, if possible, return to share them.

Captain John Burke accepted the mission without hesitation, driven by a mixture of duty and an insatiable curiosity. He had ventured to the edges of known space before, but the Rift was different. It was a mystery, an invitation, and a threat all at once. His crew, seasoned and brave, shared his resolve, though each harbored private fears about what lay within the anomaly's depths. What will come of this? In this reporters eyes nothing but disaster.

-Paul Dyson

Chapter 1: Hopes and Fears
Two Days Before the Crossing

The Rift loomed on the viewscreen, shimmering and writhing like a living thing in the vast, empty blackness of space. It was unlike anything Captain John Burke had ever seen. It pulsed with vibrant colors — shades of deep violet, piercing blue, and sickly green — twisting and merging, reaching out with invisible hands that beckoned them forward yet warned them to stay away. The Rift was dark at its core, a yawning, endless chasm that felt like it would swallow them whole if they got to close. Even from a safe distance, it seemed to breathe with a life of its own, pulling at the *Destiny*, tugging at Burke's curiosity, and stoking fear. The video log was detailed and terrifying. Recorded the first time the Destiny had seen it.

Burke sat alone in his small, dimly lit office on the bridge of the ESS *Destiny*, reviewing the mission report that lay on his tablet. It outlined what they knew so far — which, unfortunately, wasn't much. The Rift was the unexpected result of a catastrophic accident involving two ships that collided while both their tachyon drives and antimatter engines were active. The explosion had torn open the Rift, a wound in space. And it was growing. Not enough to alarm the public — not yet — but enough that Shepherd Industries, the corporation that funded the ESS *Destiny*, had sent him and his crew back to investigate.

"What do we do now?" Burke muttered under his breath, feeling the weight of the decision pressing down on him. He knew they couldn't leave the Rift unchecked; they couldn't ignore something that dangerous. But they also couldn't just blindly dive into it. He knew. He was there when it began.

His thoughts were interrupted by the chime of his office door. "Come in," he called, setting the tablet down. The door slid open to reveal Jones MacKenzie, his navigator and oldest friend, with a wry smile on his face.

"So," Jones began, leaning casually against the doorframe, "I see you're reading the mission report on... *Burke's Rift.*" He stretched out the words with a mock-grandiose tone, flashing Burke a grin.

Burke rolled his eyes. "Don't call it that, Jones. It wasn't my fault the drives exploded. I'm just glad no one was seriously hurt."

"Still, you've got a "SA" named after you. Not many captains can say that," Jones chuckled, easing himself into the chair across from Burke's desk. "Though I guess having a 'Spatial Anomaly' named after you isn't exactly the legacy most people dream of."

Burke allowed himself a small smile. He had recruited Jones for this mission six months ago, convincing him to join an experimental mission on the ESS *Destiny*, a starship unlike any other. It was one of a kind, equipped with advanced technology for deep-space exploration. The ship had been built to push boundaries, to explore the farthest reaches of space — and now, apparently, to look into spatial anomalies.

"So, what's the plan, boss?" Jones asked, his gaze growing serious as he looked at Burke intently.

Burke leaned back, considering his words. "I thought about recommending the ESS *Explorer* for the mission, but it's not ready yet. We can't afford to wait while this Rift keeps expanding. The *Destiny* is repaired, and we're ready to go in a day or two. We're the best ship for the job, Jones. We'll have take a look ourselves."

Jones raised an eyebrow. "The *Explorer* isn't finished? I didn't realize we were still Shepherd Industries 'most experimental ship,'" he replied, his tone half-joking but with an edge of concern.

Burke sighed. "Like I said, we're the best option. Besides, if this Rift is as dangerous as it looks, I trust this crew to handle it. We've been through a lot together." He glanced down at the report on his tablet again, the colors of the Rift reflecting in his eyes. "We can't let it keep growing. We've got to find a way to stop it, or at least understand it."

Jones nodded thoughtfully, but then, in true form, let his practical side show. "Well, if we're heading out tomorrow, I'd better grab a meal while I can. Care to join me?"

Burke shook his head, smiling. "Not tonight, Jones. You know Rebecca's expecting me. It's been a while since we've had dinner together without me having to rush off. She'll be waiting."

Jones gave him a knowing smile, leaning back. "Ah, the wife calls. Fair enough, Captain. You'd better keep her happy. No one wants a grumpy Mrs. Burke waiting for them at home. Another time, then."

Burke laughed, standing up and clapping Jones on the shoulder. "Another time. Now go get your dinner. I've got somewhere to be."

As they left the office, the familiar hum of the *Destiny*'s engines filled the corridor. They went their separate ways, Burke heading toward the shuttle bay hoping he was not to late.

John and Rebecca Burke's Home, Seaside, New Boston – 2366

The streets of New Boston were quiet in the evening, illuminated by the soft glow of city lights reflecting off the bay. John Burke entered his home, a modest house by the sea, and was greeted by the comforting warmth of familiarity. Above the doorway, a wooden plaque read: "Good Food, Friends, and Fun." Rebecca had hung it there when they moved in, a small reminder of the simple joys that anchored them amidst the chaos of his life in space.

"Finally!" Rebecca called from the living room, her voice carrying a playful note of irritation. She was seated on the couch, tapping her foot with a smile that betrayed her annoyance.

John grinned, moving over to join her. "I know, I know. I'm late. Work kept me longer than I planned."

Rebecca raised an eyebrow. "Burke's Rift again?"

Grimacing John nodded, sighing as he sank into the seat beside her. "They want us to go in. We're scheduled to head out tomorrow."

Rebecca's expression softened as she placed a hand on his. "Are you sure about this, John? That Rift... it is dangerous. Unknown."

"It is," he admitted. "But that's why we have to go. We can't leave something like that unchecked. It's growing, Rebecca. We don't know what it'll become."

She nodded slowly, understanding the burden he carried. "Just... come back to me, okay? I don't want to have to go in after you. I mean it. I'll take the new Explorer out if I have to!"

He leaned in, pressing his forehead against hers, taking in her familiar warmth, her presence. "I promise. And tonight, I'm here. And I believe I owe you a nice, quiet dinner."

She laughed, cautiously squeezing his hand. "Then let's go. I've been waiting for 'good food, friends, and fun' all night."

As they left the house, arm in arm, the Rift loomed in John's mind, casting a shadow over the evening. But for tonight, he chose to leave it behind, if only for a moment. Tomorrow, they would face the unknown. But tonight, he was just John, with Rebecca by his side, savoring one last peaceful evening before the journey into the void.

Chapter 2: Crossing Into the Void

The ESS *Destiny* hovered at the edge of the Rift, its sleek form outlined by the colors swirling beyond. On the bridge, every eye was fixed on the viewscreen as the ship prepared to cross into the unknown. Captain John Burke stood at the center, his gaze steely, his expression a mask of composure. But beneath the calm exterior, his heart pounded with the weight of the mission. They were about to go where no human had gone before.

"Final checks," he commanded, his voice calm but filled with the tension that crackled in the air.

"Magnetic Shields are stable," reported Grant Masters, the operations officer, his fingers dancing across his console. "Radiation levels within expected parameters, but we're definitely pushing it. The Rift is like a live wire out there."

Dr. Yamari's voice echoed from the back of the bridge. "I'll keep monitoring everyone's vitals. Radiation stress levels are already spiking across the crew."

John nodded, his jaw tight. They were as ready as they could be. He turned to Shannon O'Neil, the pilot, seated at the helm with her hands gripping the controls. Her face was set with fierce concentration, her eyes scanning every readout, every flicker of light on her console. "Wing Commander 15 for real!" She breathed under her breath.

"Steady as she goes, Lieutenant," he said, offering her a look of encouragement.

Shannon gave a terse nod, her knuckles white as she tightened her grip on the yoke. Crossing into the Rift was no ordinary maneuver. The Rift's strange energies exerted a pull that defied any calculation, an inconsistent gravitational force that tugged at the ship in unpredictable ways. Navigating the *Destiny* through such turbulence was like trying to pilot through a hurricane — only here, the storm wasn't made of wind and rain but of unstable electrical fields and fluctuating magnetic currents.

"Approaching the Rift boundary in thirty seconds," announced Jones MacKenzie, his voice steady but carrying a hint of awe as he watched the Rift's mesmerizing colors swirl on the viewscreen.

Shannon's heart raced as they neared the boundary. Every instinct screamed that she was on the edge of a cliff, about to dive into a whirlpool of unknown dangers. Her training had prepared her for deep-space maneuvers, but this was something else entirely. The controls felt heavier under her hands, as if the Rift itself was resisting her touch.

"Here we go," she muttered under her breath, steeling herself. She adjusted the pitch thrusters, fine-tuning the *Destiny*'s angle for entry, but the sensors were already flickering with error codes. The Rift's energy field was interfering with the navigation systems, blurring the lines between what was real and what the ship's sensors perceived.

Burke watched her closely. "How are you holding up, Lieutenant?"

"Systems are… reacting," she replied, trying to keep her voice calm. "But we're taking distortion hits. The Rift's radiation is bending our signals. I'm flying blind on half my readouts."

The *Destiny* shuddered as it crossed the boundary, the ship trembling like a leaf caught in a gale. Shannon gritted her teeth, forcing herself to focus on the manual controls as automatic systems began to fail, one by one. Her console flashed a cascade of warnings, and she quickly rerouted power from the auxiliary systems to stabilize the helm.

"Entering the Rift!" Jones announced as the viewscreen lit up with blinding colors.

The moment the ship crossed the threshold, the entire bridge was filled with a low, almost haunting hum that seemed to emanate from the Rift itself. The stars outside vanished, swallowed by a sea of color that twisted and pulsed. Shannon felt the controls buck beneath her hands, as if the Rift were trying to wrench the ship off course.

"Compensating for gravitational flux," she said, her voice strained as she fought to keep the ship steady. "It's… stronger than we anticipated."

Another jolt rocked the *Destiny*, sending a shockwave through the hull. Shannon struggled to correct the ship's course, her fingers flying over the controls as the Rift pulled them in multiple directions at once, each tug a different frequency and angle. It was like being trapped in the center of a vast spider's web, each thread of energy tightening around them, binding them to some chaotic rhythm.

"Magnetic Shields at eighty percent and dropping," Grant Masters reported, his tone edged with worry. "We're taking direct hits from the radiation field."

Shannon's head pounded as she fought to keep her focus. The Rift seemed to be alive, reacting to her every maneuver, twisting its energies to counteract her movements. The controls grew heavier, more resistant, as if the ship itself were sinking into a viscous sea. She glanced at her console and saw that the helm was overheating; sweat beaded on her forehead as she forced herself to stay steady.

"Captain, I'm losing responsiveness on the lateral thrusters," she said, her voice tight.

"Keep her steady, Lieutenant," Burke replied, his voice calm but firm. "You're doing fine."

"Easy for you to say," she muttered, gritting her teeth as she leaned into the controls. The ship veered slightly to the right, caught by an unexpected current of graviton particles. She adjusted the trajectory manually, her eyes locked on the chaotic patterns outside, searching for any visual anchor point, anything that might help guide them through the Rift's ever-shifting landscape.

Just then, the *Destiny* jolted violently to the side, throwing O'Neil against her harness. A surge of energy washed over the ship, distorting the viewscreen in a blur of colors and shadows.

Shannon gasped, wrestling with the controls. "We're getting pushed deeper in. It's like something's... pulling us."

"Captain, energy flux is destabilizing the core," Connor Vincente's voice crackled over the comm from Engineering. "The Rift's interference is overwhelming the tachyon drive. I can't keep it stable for much longer!"

"Hold it together, Connor," Burke ordered, his gaze intense. "Divert power as needed. Shannon, can you maintain course?"

"I'm trying!" Shannon barked, her heart pounding. The Rift seemed to be testing her, pulling at the ship with invisible hands that gripped the *Destiny* tighter with each passing second. She adjusted the stabilizers again, rerouting power from non-essential systems to keep the ship from veering off course.

But the Rift had other plans. Another surge of energy slammed into the *Destiny*, and the controls slipped in her hands. Shannon felt the ship lurch to the left, twisting under the pressure of the wave. Alarms blared around her as the guidance systems flickered, sensors screaming in protest. She was fighting a battle on two fronts: the *Destiny*'s own systems, struggling to compensate, and the relentless pull of the Rift, dragging them further into its depths.

"Captain," she said, her voice shaking slightly as she gripped the yoke with all her strength, "I don't know how much longer I can hold this course. The Rift... it's adapting. It's like it knows our every move."

Burke's jaw clenched, his eyes fixed on the swirling chaos outside. "Just a little longer, Shannon. Get us to the designated coordinates. Once we're through, we can stabilize."

Shannon's fingers burned from the friction of the controls, her muscles aching as she forced the ship back on course. She could feel the Rift's pull, a force that seemed almost sentient, twisting around her, challenging her skill, testing her limits. But she wasn't about to let it win.

"Almost... there," she whispered, her voice barely audible as she locked in the final coordinates. With a final push, she guided the *Destiny* through the last stretch, the viewscreen filled with a blinding flash of light as they pierced through the core of the Rift.

And then, silence.

The Rift's chaotic colors faded, replaced by an empty void, a vast, unsettling darkness that stretched endlessly in every direction. The ship was stable, floating in the stillness, as if the universe itself were holding its breath.

Shannon exhaled, her hands shaking as she released the controls. Her heart was still racing, but she had done it. They had crossed into the Void.

Burke placed a hand on her shoulder, his voice low but filled with quiet pride. "You did it, Shannon. Well done."

She managed a weak smile, her breath coming in short gasps. "Thanks, Captain. But... whatever's in here... it's watching us. I can feel it."

Outside, the darkness loomed, vast and unknowable, as the *Destiny* struggled to hold it's position in the Void. The Rift had let them through, but Shannon knew that whatever awaited them here was just beginning.

Chapter 3: A Captain's Burden

John Burke stood in the center of the *Destiny*'s bridge, his gaze fixed on the endless darkness stretching beyond the viewscreen. The Void was like nothing he had ever seen, an expanse devoid of stars, color, or light, a seemingly infinite abyss. It was as if they'd crossed into a place that even the universe itself had abandoned.

He tightened his grip on the railing, steadying himself. He was the captain of this vessel, and his crew depended on him to guide them through the unknown. But there, in the deepest corner of his mind, a nagging fear took root. It was the kind of fear he would never speak of, one that he kept buried beneath layers of duty and resolve.

He might not see Rebecca again.

Burke exhaled slowly, pushing the thought aside. There was no time to let personal worries distract him. He'd brought his wife to the *Destiny*'s launch six months ago, and he still remembered her bright, reassuring smile as they parted. "Take care of yourself, John," she'd told him, her fingers brushing against his. "Come back to me."

"Captain?" Grant Masters, his operations officer, broke through his reverie. "Scanners are showing nothing in any direction. It's... complete emptiness. No light, no mass, no radiation signatures. It's as if space itself just ends here."

Burke's jaw tightened. "Keep scanning, Mr. Masters. Whatever this Void is, there's something on the other side. We just need to find it."

He could feel his crew's eyes on him, each of them searching for any hint of doubt in his expression. If he faltered, if he even let them suspect he was rattled, the entire mission could unravel. "Burke's Rift" was partly his responsibility — even though he hated to admit it. There had to be a way to close it.

"Shields are holding steady, Captain," Connor Vincente called from Engineering over the comm. "But the Rift's energy seems to have left a residue on our hull. It's not dangerous, at least not immediately, but we should monitor it."

"Understood," Burke replied. "Keep me informed of any changes."

The bridge felt colder here in the Void, as if the darkness itself had seeped into the walls of the *Destiny*. He glanced around at his officers. Shannon O'Neil, their pilot, sat quietly at the helm, her fingers still tense from the battle with the Rift's pull. She was tough, determined, but he could see the fatigue in her eyes. Behind her, Jones MacKenzie worked his station with a focused, almost obsessive precision. MacKenzie's calm demeanor was comforting, but Burke knew his old friend well enough to sense the underlying tension.

Burke took a deep breath and addressed the crew. "We've entered an uncharted territory, something no one has ever seen before. Our mission is to explore, to understand, and to survive. But remember: we're not here to conquer this place. We're here to learn. Keep your minds sharp and your wits about you."

He glanced at each of them, holding their gazes for a moment, hoping to communicate strength, stability. If they believed he was certain, then maybe they would be, too.

Inside, though, a small part of him felt the weight of isolation. Rebecca's face drifted into his mind again. He remembered their last dinner together, the quiet conversations, the feeling of her hand in his. She had understood his call to duty, but the thought of never returning to her, of leaving her alone — it was an ache he couldn't shake. And here, in the Void, with nothing familiar around him, that ache grew sharper.

"Captain," Dr. Yamari's voice came through the comm, pulling him back to reality. "I'd like to do a full health scan of the crew. The Void's environment is... unknown, and I want to make sure everyone's still functioning at optimal levels."

"Good call, Doctor," Burke replied. "Coordinate with Grant to make sure all data is logged."

He couldn't afford to lose focus. Each decision he made now could mean the difference between survival and catastrophe. His crew needed him steady, composed, decisive. Every order had to be clear, every plan airtight. They had entered the Rift as explorers, but here, in the endless black, he knew they had to be something else now: survivors.

"Mr. MacKenzie," he said, turning to his navigation officer, "do we have any sense of direction here?"

MacKenzie shook his head, frustration evident in his eyes. "Without any fixed stars or points of reference, I can't give you a precise heading, Captain. I can plot theoretical paths based on our last known course, but there's no way to confirm where we're going. It's like... like trying to navigate through fog with no compass."

Burke nodded. "Understood. Keep a steady course. If there's an exit, we'll find it."

But he knew the truth: they were adrift, lost in the Void. For the first time in his career, he had no clear sense of where they were or how to get home. It was an uncomfortable feeling, the vulnerability gnawing at him.

He turned to Shannon, his voice low and steady. "Lieutenant O'Neil, prepare for a short burst from the anti-matter engines. Let's see if we can find any variation in the space around us."

Shannon looked up, her expression serious. "Aye, Captain. I'll keep it gentle; wouldn't want to upset the locals, if there are any."

Burke managed a faint smile at her attempt to lighten the mood. It was a small gesture, but it reminded him that they weren't machines. His crew was human, and they needed a leader who remembered that. The pressures of command, the constant calculations, the worry — he couldn't let it erase his humanity. They weren't alone in the Void; they had each other.

The ship shuddered slightly as Shannon engaged the engines, and the *Destiny* lurched forward, inching deeper into the darkness. The hum of the engines reverberated through the bridge, filling the silence with a steady, reassuring sound. Burke listened to it, grounding himself in the familiarity of his ship.

But then, from the corner of his eye, he noticed something strange. A flicker on the viewscreen, a shimmer in the dark.

"Captain," Jones said, his voice cautious, "I'm picking up... something. A faint energy reading. It's barely there, but... it's not natural."

Burke leaned forward, his pulse quickening. This could be their first real encounter with whatever lay in the Void, their first clue to its mysteries. But he also knew that discovery often came with danger.

"Bring it up on the viewscreen," he ordered.

As the image enhanced, they saw a distant, faint glow — like a distant star, barely discernible, surrounded by wisps of something almost organic, pulsating slowly in the darkness.

"Looks like we're not alone, after all," Shannon whispered, her fingers tightening on the controls.

Burke's stomach twisted with anticipation and unease. The glow was beautiful, mesmerizing, but he sensed a hidden danger lurking beneath its surface. As captain, he had to make a decision, and quickly. Do they investigate this anomaly or attempt to chart a course away from it? The safety of his crew depended on him choosing wisely.

For a fleeting moment, Rebecca's face crossed his mind again, her smile soft and reassuring. He had promised her he'd come back. And to keep that promise, he had to make the right choices here in the Void.

"Steady, everyone," he said, his voice strong and unwavering. "We're going to approach carefully. Keep all sensors active and weapons at the ready. Let's see what we're dealing with."

As they edged toward the glow, Burke felt the weight of his responsibility settle even heavier on his shoulders. The Void was a place of unknowns, a trial that would test every ounce of his strength, every fiber of his resolve. He would lead his crew through it, no matter the cost.

Chapter 4: Into the Unknown

The *Destiny* crept forward, edging closer to the strange glow in the Void. On the bridge, the air was thick with tension. Each member of the crew was at their station, every eye focused on the mysterious light that flickered like a phantom in the darkness.

Captain Burke felt a chill as he studied the viewscreen. This strange glow was the only sign of anything tangible in the Void so far. But it was something, and that was enough to demand their attention. His instincts screamed at him to be cautious, but the curiosity that had driven him through his career whispered that this might be the discovery of a lifetime.

"Grant," he said, turning to his operations officer, "I need a full analysis. What do we know about this... unknown?"

Grant Masters, always meticulous, ran his hands over his console, frowning as he tried to interpret the sensor readings. "Captain, it's not like anything we've seen before. It has a faint energy signature, but it's fluctuating. Whatever it is, it's emitting low-level tachyon particles, but... it's strange. Unstable."

"Unstable in what way?" Burke asked.

"It's like the energy is... rippling, shifting," Masters replied. "Almost as if it's trying to take form or... communicate."

Burke's mind raced. They were deep into uncharted space, a dimension beyond the known universe. The rift had brought them here, but no one knew what "here" really was. And now, this flickering light — this possible life form — was signaling... something.

"Keep monitoring it, but don't engage," Burke ordered. "We're just observing for now."

At the helm, Shannon O'Neil's fingers danced over the controls. Her brow was furrowed in concentration, her eyes unblinking as she steered the *Destiny* closer, yet kept a safe distance. She was a stellar pilot, Burke knew, but even she seemed shaken. After their rough entry through the rift, she was well aware of the risks of piloting the ship through this strange space.

"Steady, Lieutenant," Burke said quietly, noticing her tension.

"I know, Captain," Shannon replied, her voice just above a whisper. "It's just... I've never delt with anything like this."

Suddenly, a faint voice crackled over the comm, startling everyone on the bridge. It was distorted, broken by static, as if someone was speaking to them from another universe.

"D... Des...ny... hear... me..."

Burke froze, his heart pounding. The voice was human, unmistakably so, but garbled and weak. He looked at Grant, who was furiously adjusting the comms frequency, trying to clean up the signal.

"This is Captain John Burke of the ESS *Destiny*," Burke said, his voice clear and firm. "Identify yourself."

Silence. The voice disappeared as quickly as it had come, leaving only a faint hiss of static in its place. Burke clenched his fists, straining to hear any hint of a response, but there was nothing.

"Did you catch that?" he asked, looking to Grant.

Masters nodded, his face pale. "Captain... I swear, that voice sounded familiar. But there's no logical way anyone else would be out here."

Burke felt a pang of dread. The Void was supposed to be empty, devoid of any known life or objects. So who — or what — had just called out to them? And why did that voice stir a familiarity, an echo of something he couldn't quite place?

He took a deep breath, trying to push the eerie feeling away. "Keep monitoring the frequency," he ordered. "If they try to reach us again, I want to be ready."

"Understood, sir," Masters replied, but he still looked shaken. The entire crew was on edge now, the mysterious voice sending chills through them all.

Burke looked over at Jones MacKenzie, his old friend and navigator. Jones gave him a nod, steady and reassuring, as if to say, "I've got your back." It was a small comfort, but Burke needed it. The weight of command felt heavier with each passing moment.

Turning back to the viewscreen, Burke focused on the glow in the distance. The faint flicker was drawing them in, as if it were reaching out, inviting them — or warning them. Either way, Burke knew they had to approach it with caution. But the allure of the unknown was undeniable.

"Lieutenant O'Neil," he said, "bring us closer, but keep shields at maximum and prepare for evasive maneuvers if necessary."

"Aye, Captain," Shannon replied, her voice steely. She engaged the thrusters, inching the *Destiny* forward, the ship gliding through the Void like a echo in the night.

As they approached, the glow became more pronounced, its light casting eerie shadows across the bridge. It pulsed in rhythmic waves, almost like a heartbeat. It was hypnotic, beautiful in its strange, alien way, yet deeply unsettling. Burke's instincts screamed that this was no ordinary phenomenon — it was something ancient, something powerful.

A new sensor alert chimed, and Connor Vincente's voice came through the comms, tight with urgency. "Captain, I'm reading a massive energy buildup around the unknown. It's spiking — whatever it is, it's waking up!"

"Evasive maneuvers, now!" Burke barked, his voice sharp.

Shannon's hands flew over the controls as she spun the *Destiny* to port, veering away from the glowing entity. The ship lurched, engines straining, as a sudden wave of energy surged out from the anomaly, sweeping over them. The bridge lights flickered, and a low, ominous hum reverberated through the hull.

Burke gripped the railing, bracing himself. "Damage report!"

Connor's voice crackled through, tense but controlled. "Minor hull breaches in sectors seven and eight, but nothing critical. Shields absorbed most of the impact. But whatever that thing is, it's powerful. I'd recommend we keep our distance, sir."

Burke nodded, heart pounding. "Understood. Pull us back, Lieutenant O'Neil. We're not taking any more chances with that... thing."

As they retreated, the glow gradually dimmed, its pulsing slowing until it faded back into the darkness. The bridge fell silent, the only sound the faint hum of the engines and the labored breathing of the crew.

Burke took a deep breath, steadying himself. The Void was not just an empty expanse — it was alive, unpredictable, and dangerous. Whatever they had encountered was a reminder that they were out of their depth, navigating forces they didn't understand.

He looked around the bridge, meeting the eyes of each of his officers. They were shaken, but they were still here, still following him. It was his job to keep it that way, no matter the cost.

"Alright, everyone," he said, his voice calm but resolute. "We've gotten a taste of what this place has to offer. Let's regroup, analyze the data, and figure out our next move. We're not leaving until we understand what we're dealing with. But remember, our priority is survival."

As he spoke, the image of Rebecca drifted into his mind once more. Her smile, her laugh, the way she'd always believed in him. She was his anchor, his reason to find a way out of this void and back to the life they had together.

He wouldn't let her down.

"Let's get to work," he said, turning back to the viewscreen, his resolve hardening.

The Void might be, dark, and filled with mysteries, but Captain John Burke knew it was only dark and mysterious till it wasn't.

Chapter 5: The Message in the Light

The bridge of the *ESS Destiny* was bathed in the eerie, pulsing light coming from the object floating in the void ahead. For days, this bright, persistent glow had hovered just outside their ship, unchanging and seemingly waiting. The crew had tried to keep their distance, cautious of its unknown origin and purpose, but the light was hard to ignore. It seeped into their minds, whispering curiosity and apprehension in equal measure.

Captain John Burke had assembled his senior officers on the bridge to discuss what, exactly, they were dealing with. The object had become an undeniable enigma in the endless darkness of the Void, and the crew's nerves were on edge.

"Grant, what do we know about that thing?" Burke asked, keeping his gaze fixed on the strange light.

Grant Masters, the *Destiny*'s operations officer, frowned at his console, scrolling through various scans and readings they'd taken over the past few hours. "It's still emitting a low-level signal, Captain. No detectable life signs, no obvious weapon signatures. Just... light. It's like nothing I've ever seen."

Burke nodded thoughtfully. The light was alluring in its simplicity, but something about it felt... purposeful. It wasn't random, he was sure of that. He leaned forward, his mind racing with possibilities.

"What if it's some kind of beacon?" he mused aloud. "Something left here by... whoever, or whatever, lives in the Void."

Shannon O'Neil, the pilot, turned her chair to face him, a hint of trepidation in her eyes. "Captain, with all due respect, a beacon left by whom? So far, we haven't seen any sign of life. Just silence, darkness... and now this."

Burke didn't have an answer. The Void was an empty, desolate place, yet here was this single point of light, like a lighthouse in a storm, beckoning them. "We're not going to learn anything by staying away from it. Grant, can you run a diagnostic scan on the object? Find out if it's attempting to communicate with us."

Grant nodded and initiated a deep scan. His console began to fill with lines of data, unreadable to anyone else but instantly meaningful to him. His brow furrowed as he analyzed the information coming in.

"It's... strange, Captain," he said, eyes narrowing. "It's like this thing is actively probing our systems. It's attempting to establish a data link—trying to interface with our communications network."

Burke straightened, intrigued but wary. "Trying to communicate with us? Are you sure?"

"Positive," Grant replied. "It's not transmitting in any language we recognize, but there's a pattern to it. I'd say it's a message of some kind... a structured series of signals repeating over and over, almost like a handshake protocol. It's as if it's waiting for us to accept the connection."

The bridge went quiet. This was not a simple object, nor was it just a light floating in the dark. It was intelligent, or at least created by something intelligent. And it wanted to talk.

"Captain, I don't like this," Shannon said, her voice a low murmur. "We have no idea who—or what—made that thing. If we let it connect to our systems, there's no telling what could happen."

Burke weighed her words carefully. She was right, of course. They were explorers, not fools. But in his gut, he felt an unshakable pull—a need to understand.

"We can't ignore this," he finally said, his tone resolute. "If it's a message, it could hold answers to what the Void is and why this place feels... so alien. We can't turn our backs on the chance to learn."

Grant nodded, already beginning preparations for a controlled connection. "I'll set up a restricted network link, something isolated from our main systems. If it tries to access anything beyond that, I can shut it down immediately."

Burke appreciated Grant's caution. "Good thinking. Proceed with the link. Let's see what this thing has to say."

The crew watched anxiously as Grant activated the connection. A moment later, the bright light flared, filling the bridge with an intense, blinding radiance. Burke shielded his eyes, feeling a strange warmth from the light—a warmth that seemed to pulse in rhythm with his heartbeat.

Then, as quickly as it had brightened, the light dimmed. A low hum filled the air, resonating through the ship's walls and decks. Symbols and foreign text appeared on Grant's console, flickering as the object's message began to translate into something recognizable.

"It's working," Grant said, his voice tinged with awe. "The object... it's transmitting a message. And it's adapting to our language protocols, restructuring itself so we can understand."

The bridge crew leaned in, captivated as the symbols on the console began to form coherent phrases. Slowly, a message took shape—a series of broken sentences, disjointed but decipherable.

"Warning. Boundary breach. You are in forbidden space. Voidless... not human... exist here. They... watch. They... hunger."

Burke felt a chill run down his spine as he read the words. The Void was not empty; it was not merely a strange dimension. Something lived here, something that the creators of this beacon had feared enough to leave a warning.

"Captain, it's not done," Grant said, pointing to the console as more text continued to scroll. **"This beacon... last defense. Interface with... your vessel... essential. Information relay... protect you... from Voidless."**

"Protect us?" Shannon said, her voice laced with disbelief. "Protect us from the Voidless?"

Burke's mind spun as he tried to make sense of the message. "This beacon... it's not just a warning. It's a lifeline. Whoever left it, they wanted us to have the means to survive here."

But as soon as he said it, doubt crept in. If the beacon needed to interface with the *Destiny* to protect them, then the situation might be even more dangerous than they'd realized. It wasn't just a warning—it was an active defense mechanism. This beacon, this light, was designed to be their shield in a hostile dimension.

"Grant, how is it trying to interface with our systems?" Burke asked, his voice tense.

Grant's fingers flew over his console as he examined the interface logs. "It's trying to integrate with our navigation and sensor arrays. I think it wants to map our surroundings, maybe to detect any of those... entities it warned us about."

Burke considered the risks. Allowing a foreign object to access their systems went against every protocol, but this was no ordinary situation. If they rejected the interface, they might be left defenseless in the Void, with no way of detecting whatever dangers lurked out there.

He looked around at his crew, reading the fear and uncertainty in their eyes. "I know this is risky," he said, addressing them all, "but I believe we're meant to use this beacon. It was left here for a reason. We need its protection if we're going to make it out of this place alive."

Shannon sighed, visibly uneasy but resigned. "Then let's do it, Captain. We're already in deep. Might as well see it through."

Grant nodded, initiating a deeper connection with the beacon. As he did, the light pulsed again, brighter and stronger, and the humming grew louder, vibrating through the *Destiny's* hull.

On the screen, more text appeared, instructions detailing a set of defensive protocols. It was a map of sorts—a way to avoid triggering the attention of the entities that resided here. The beacon's creators had left a path, a guide to survive the Void.

"Stay silent. Avoid... energy surges. Voidless sense... life force. Follow coordinates... escape vector."

The bridge was silent as everyone absorbed the gravity of the message. They were not alone in the Void, and the things that dwelled here could sense them, track them, even hunt them.

"Set a course for those coordinates," Burke ordered, his voice steady, though his heart raced. "And make sure every system is running at minimum output. Let's stay as silent as possible."

Shannon input the coordinates provided by the beacon, her hands steady despite the fear they all felt. As the *Destiny* began to drift slowly through the Void, following the beacon's guidance, Burke couldn't shake the feeling that they were being watched.

"Captain," Grant said, his voice a near-whisper. "I think... I think it's helping us. The beacon. Whoever left it—they wanted someone to survive this place."

Burke nodded, feeling a deep sense of gratitude for these unknown benefactors. "Let's hope their instructions get us out of here."

The *Destiny* moved through the Void, silent and cautious, its systems dimmed and subdued. Outside, the light of the beacon shone ahead of them, guiding them through the darkness.

As they drifted deeper, Burke felt the faintest flicker of hope. They were not alone. There were others who had come before, others who had fought to survive the unknown. And now, their legacy was lighting the path for the *Destiny* and its crew.

But Burke knew one thing for certain—the Void was not empty. And whatever was watching them would not give up easily.

Chapter 6: Rebecca's Resolve

Rebecca Burke sat alone in her office at the Shepherd Industries headquarters, her gaze fixed on the endless stretch of stars visible through the floor-to-ceiling windows. The gleaming towers of New Boston stretched below her, their lights twinkling like stars of their own. But her heart and mind were light-years away, drifting somewhere out in the cosmos alongside her husband, John Burke.

He'd been gone too long.

At first, it was just the typical communication delays. Shepherd Industries had briefed her on what to expect once the *ESS Destiny* entered deep space; messages would take days, even weeks, to come through. But now silence had swallowed everything. It had been over a month since her last message from John. He reported about the strange—shimmering Rift, being dark and incomprehensible. The last words he'd sent her were disturbing: *"Don't worry, Rebecca. I'll be back before you know it."*

That was a month ago.

Rebecca closed her eyes, taking a deep breath as she fought against the wave of worry that threatened to crash over her. Her father, Micah Shepherd, had insisted that John would be fine. He'd argued that no news was good news and that the *Destiny*'s crew were highly skilled, all capable of handling the dangers of deep space exploration.

But Rebecca knew better. She knew John. And she knew, deep down, that something was wrong.

Standing from her desk, she walked over to the model of the *ESS Explorer*, the newest starship designed by Shepherd Industries. It was sleek and strong, built with the latest technologies and outfitted to withstand even the harshest conditions of space. The *Explorer* was meant to follow in the *Destiny*'s path, another leap forward for humanity's journey into the stars. But it was still weeks away from completion, a half-finished colossus waiting in the shipyards.

For the past few months, Rebecca had poured herself into overseeing the *Explorer*'s construction, throwing herself into every detail. She'd spent endless hours working on the ship, talking to engineers, testing systems, and pushing for efficiency. This was her way of being close to him—building something that would one day join the *Destiny* in the stars.

But now, she was done waiting. Done with the reassurances, done with pretending everything was fine. She had resources, she had knowledge, and she had a nearly finished starship waiting in the dry docks. And most of all, she had a promise to keep.

Her fingers traced over the model's hull, and she made her decision.

It was time to bring John home!

Rebecca found her father in his private office, looking over financial reports on his holoscreen. Micah Shepherd was a man who commanded every room he entered—sturdy, with silver hair and sharp eyes that never missed a thing. He glanced up as she entered, one eyebrow raised in curiosity.

"Rebecca," he said, setting aside his holoscreen. "What brings you here at this hour?"

She didn't waste any time with pleasantries. "I'm taking the *Explorer*," she said, her tone as unyielding as the titanium hull of the starship.

Micah's eyes narrowed, and a slight frown appeared on his face. "What do you mean you're taking the *Explorer*? It's not ready, Rebecca. We still have months of work left. Systems checks, weapons calibrations—"

"Then we'll accelerate the schedule," she interrupted, crossing her arms. "The ship is close enough. It doesn't need to be perfect; it just needs to be functional."

Micah stood, placing his hands on the desk. "I understand you're worried about John, but you can't just hijack an unfinished starship and fly off into the Rift. Do you have any idea how dangerous that would be?"

Rebecca met his gaze, her eyes blazing with determination. "Do you have any idea how dangerous it was for *Destiny*? We sent them out there without fully understanding the consequences. Now John and his crew are stranded, and we're just sitting here, hoping for a miracle."

Micah sighed, running a hand through his silver hair. "Rebecca... I know you love him, but sometimes you have to trust that the people out there know what they're doing. John is the best captain I've ever met. He's resilient, smart. If anyone can make it through this, it's him."

Her jaw tightened. "And if he's still out there, he'll need help. I'm not going to sit here and do nothing, Dad. I'm not going to be the helpless wife who waits at home, hoping for a message that may never come."

Micah looked at her, the weight of his years visible in his expression. He'd raised Rebecca to be strong, to be a leader, to think for herself. He knew he couldn't simply talk her out of this. But the idea of sending his daughter out into the unknown was almost unbearable.

"Rebecca," he said softly, "the *Explorer* isn't just a ship. It's a prototype, an investment, a billion-credit project. If you take it, and something happens..."

She took a step forward, placing her hand on his arm. "Dad, please. I need to do this. I need to know I did everything I could to bring him home."

A long silence fell between them, and Micah looked down, visibly struggling. Finally, he nodded, though his face was lined with worry.

"Alright," he said, his voice low. "But you're not going alone. I'll gather a skeleton crew, the best engineers and navigators we have. If you're doing this, you're doing it with support."

Relief washed over her, but she maintained her composure. "Thank you."

"But know this, Rebecca," he continued, his eyes hardening. "If I think, for one moment, that the risks are too high, I will bring you back. No arguments. I won't lose you too."

She nodded, understanding the gravity of his words. "Understood."

Within days, the *ESS Explorer* was as ready as it would ever be. Rebecca had handpicked the crew herself—seasoned engineers, navigators, and operations officers who knew the risks and were willing to join her. The starship still lacked the full capabilities it would eventually have, but it was enough to get them where they needed to go.

As she stood on the bridge, staring out at the shipyard, she couldn't help but feel a mixture of nerves and anticipation. The

Explorer was her ship now, her responsibility. But this was about more than duty—it was personal. She would find John. She would bring him home.

Her second-in-command, Commander Alex Rivera, stepped up beside her. "All systems are as stable as they're going to get, Captain," he reported. "We're ready to depart on your command."

"Thank you, Commander," she replied, feeling a surge of gratitude for the support of her crew. They all understood the risks, yet here they were, willing to follow her into the unknown.

She took a deep breath, steeling herself. This was it. This was her chance to rewrite the ending, to save the man she loved.

"Set course for the Rift," she ordered, her voice steady. "Let's bring them home."

As the *Explorer* powered up, the familiar hum of the engines filled the bridge. The stars stretched out before them, an endless frontier, filled with both danger and hope. Rebecca felt the weight of the unknown pressing down on her, but she welcomed it. This was her mission now. And nothing—not the darkness of the Void, not the warnings, and certainly not her own fear—would stop her.

The *ESS Explorer* surged forward, heading toward the Rift that had swallowed the *Destiny* whole. Rebecca Burke's heart beat steadily, a rhythm that matched her resolve.

Chapter 7: Following the Light

The void pressed down on them like a weight, an all-encompassing darkness that seemed to stretch into infinity. Jones Mackenzie, Navigator of the *ESS Destiny*, had thought he'd been trained to handle anything deep space could throw at him, but nothing in all his years of training had prepared him for this—a vast, empty blackness that seemed to eat away at light, sound, and even time itself.

Jones sat at the navigation console, staring intently at the screen as he tried to make sense of the information in front of him. The bright beacon they'd initially thought was just an unknown—a strange, shining light floating out there in the depths—had turned out to be something else entirely. After extensive analysis by Dr. Yamari and the science team, they'd discovered it was a message buoy, or perhaps more accurately, an ancient probe designed to interface with other ships' systems. Its design was unfamiliar, alien, but somehow it had recognized the *Destiny*, offering an escape route from the void.

For Jones, the revelation had been both a relief and a new source of stress. The buoy had transmitted a complex series of coordinates and instructions, guiding them through what appeared to be a narrow path toward the edge of the void. But the route was anything but simple; it twisted and turned in ways that defied every rule of space navigation he knew. And every time he veered even slightly off course, the systems began to malfunction, as if the ship itself was warning him that he was drifting too far.

Jones ran a hand through his short, dark hair, trying to keep his nerves under control. The problem wasn't just that the path was difficult—it was that the void around them seemed to shift and change, like it was a living, breathing thing. Each step along the route had to be perfect, or they'd risk getting lost in the void forever or falling prey to the Voidless!

"Jones, how are we doing up there?" Captain Burke's voice crackled through the comm.

Jones exhaled and tapped his headset. "Making progress, Captain," he replied, trying to keep his voice steady. "But... this isn't like anything I've seen before. Every coordinate from the buoy's message has to be followed exactly, or it just leads us into more darkness."

There was a pause on the other end, and Jones could almost feel Burke's worry. "I trust you, Jones. You're the best navigator I know. If anyone can get us out of here, it's you."

Those words should have been reassuring, but they only added to the pressure Jones already felt. He was responsible for everyone on the ship—the crew, the Captain, his friends. If he made a mistake, if he misread even a single coordinate, they'd be lost forever.

"Thanks, Captain," Jones said, though he wasn't sure how confident he sounded.

He looked back at the strange pattern of coordinates and instructions that glowed on his screen. He felt like a mouse following crumbs through a labyrinth, never sure if he was getting closer to the exit or to a trap.

Beside him, Connor Vincente, the engineer, was working hard to keep the *Destiny*'s systems stable. The ship itself seemed to protest against each turn they made, each slight shift in course. Power levels fluctuated, systems flickered on and off, and at times the artificial gravity felt like it might just shut off altogether.

"How's it going, Connor?" Jones asked, glancing over at him.

Connor's face was tense, beads of sweat on his brow as he tapped away on his console. "Barely holding together. Every time we adjust course, it's like the entire ship groans. Whatever this void is, it doesn't want us to leave."

Jones nodded grimly. "Feels like it's trying to pull us back in every time we take a step forward."

Another turn came up on the navigational path—an angle that felt so wrong, so counterintuitive that every instinct in Jones's body told him not to follow it. But he couldn't question the buoy's directions. If he veered off course, he knew they'd be swallowed by the darkness.

Taking a deep breath, he adjusted the ship's course, following the buoy's instructions to the letter. The *Destiny*'s frame creaked and shuddered in protest, but it held.

Jones's hands shook as he tightened his grip on the console. "Come on, come on... just stay with me..."

He glanced at the buoy on the screen. It pulsed with a steady glow, as if encouraging him, or perhaps watching him. There was an intelligence behind its design—an intent. Someone, or something, had built it and sent it out here. Why? For whom? And why did it seem to know exactly how to navigate this impossible place?

"Whoever designed this thing... they knew how to get out of here," Jones muttered, half to himself.

Connor looked over at him. "Let's hope they were right."

With each maneuver, Jones felt the weight of the crew's lives pressing down on him. Every breath he took felt shallow, strained. The void's silence was oppressive, almost like it was pressing in on his ears. He wanted to scream, to break the silence, but he held it back. He couldn't afford to lose control now.

"Jones, are we on course?" came Captain Burke's voice again.

"Barely, but yes," Jones replied. "The buoy's directions are... strange. But they're working. Just need to keep following them."

"Good. Keep at it," Burke replied, his voice a steady anchor. "We're all counting on you."

Jones nodded, though Burke couldn't see him. The Captain's calm resolve gave him strength. He remembered all the times he'd served under Burke, the countless adventures they'd faced together. This was different—there was no enemy, no danger they could see, but that only made the fear worse. Here, the enemy was the unknown itself. And what were the Voidless? He shuddered to think.

Time felt meaningless. Hours passed, or perhaps it was minutes. The only thing that grounded him was the steady rhythm of the buoy's signal, guiding him forward through the darkness. With each new turn, each new twist, he felt a glimmer of hope, as if maybe, just maybe, they were finally getting closer to the edge

But then the path grew narrower, the coordinates more precise. The buoy's instructions demanded even tighter maneuvers, and Jones's hands grew slick with sweat as he tried to keep up. One wrong move, one tiny error, and they'd be lost again.

"Almost there," he whispered, his voice a prayer more than a statement.

And then, just as his exhaustion was about to overtake him, the buoy sent a final pulse—a brilliant flash of light that illuminated the void around them, momentarily breaking through the darkness.

In that instant, Jones saw something that took his breath away: a faint, shimmering outline of the universe beyond, as if the walls of the void were finally peeling back, allowing them to see the stars they'd longed for.

He couldn't help but smile, a rare, genuine smile that he hadn't felt in what seemed like ages.

"We're almost there," he said, louder this time, his voice filled with hope. "We're almost free."

But then he saw them...the Voidless! The view screen was filled by them. Blocking Destiny's path out and home!

Chapter 8: Dark Matter Predators

"Captain to the bridge!" Shannon O'Neil's voice rang through the comm system, edged with urgency.

Captain John Burke felt his pulse quicken. He was already on his way, sprinting down the narrow corridor toward the bridge. They had barely managed to navigate the treacherous path through the void, following the buoy's strange coordinates, and he had been holding his breath the whole time, hoping they'd be led somewhere... safe. Or at least out of the oppressive blackness.

As he burst onto the bridge, his eyes went straight to the viewscreen. Outside the *Destiny*, something strange loomed in the darkness—a shimmer, like ripples on a pond, but twisted into shapes that flickered and pulsed, shifting as if alive.

"All stop!" Burke commanded, gripping the back of Jones Mackenzie's chair to steady himself.

The ship shuddered slightly as the engines halted, the *Destiny* drifting silently within the void. Everyone on the bridge was tense, their gazes fixed on the strange shapes outside. They were close—too close—and surrounding the ship, encircling them like predators sizing up their prey.

"Scan those... things," Burke ordered, his voice steady despite the apprehension clawing at his insides. "What are they?"

Grant was already at the scanner controls, his fingers moving deftly over the interface. The bridge was silent, the crew holding their breath as they waited for the readings. After a few tense moments, the results appeared on Grant's screen, and his brow furrowed as he read them. "The Voidless!"

"Captain," Grant began, his voice low, "they're... they're some kind of life forms. Feeding on dark matter."

Burke's eyes widened. "Feeding on dark matter? I didn't think that was even possible."

Grant nodded, though his face was pale. "Neither did I, sir. But these creatures... it's like they're adapted to the void, thriving in it. They consume dark matter, keeping the balance of the energy fields around them." He paused, swallowing hard. "And the Rift—it disrupted that balance. The explosion from the tachyon drive... it must've blown out their food source. They're starving."

Burke took a deep breath, staring at the creatures outside. The way they moved was both beautiful and terrifying, their forms undulating like shadows given life. He could see the hunger in the way they circled the *Destiny*, drifting closer with each passing moment, as if they were assessing the ship, testing its defenses.

"Do you think they see us as food?" he asked, his voice barely more than a whisper.

Jones glanced up at him, his expression grim. "Possibly, Captain. If they're starving, they might see us as their only option."

Burke clenched his fists, his mind racing. These creatures were massive—larger than the *Destiny* itself. Their bodies were like twisted ribbons of darkness, with flickers of strange, iridescent light running along their edges. They had no recognizable features, no eyes or mouths that he could see, but there was a predatory intelligence in the way they moved, circling tighter and tighter.

Shannon O'Neil, the pilot, turned to Burke, her face taut with worry. "Captain, if they decide to attack, I don't know if we can outrun them. The engines are still recovering from the journey through the void."

Burke nodded, thinking hard. They had to find a way to communicate with these creatures, to show them that the *Destiny* wasn't a source of sustenance. But how could they reason with beings that fed on something as intangible as dark matter?

"Grant, do we have any records of species like these? Anything in the archives that could tell us how to communicate with them?" Burke asked, his voice tight.

Grant shook his head. "Not that I know of, sir. These creatures...the "Voidless" as the light buoy called them... they're unlike anything we've encountered. It's possible that no one else has ever seen them and lived to tell the tale."

Dr. Yamari, who had joined the bridge, leaned over the sensor console, studying the readings. "Captain, if these creatures feed on dark matter, the Rift we created could have decimated their ecosystem. They're not just hungry—they're desperate."

Burke's heart sank as he took in her words. This wasn't just a threat; it was a tragedy. These creatures were only trying to survive in a world that *Destiny*'s own actions had inadvertently destroyed.

"Options, people," Burke said, his tone sharp as he tried to rein in his worry. "How do we get out of this without becoming dinner?"

Connor Vincente, the ship's engineer, chimed in, his voice hesitant. "Captain, if they're looking for dark matter... maybe we can give them some."

Burke raised an eyebrow. "Go on."

Connor shifted uncomfortably but continued, "Our power core interacts with dark matter particles to generate energy. If we could create a controlled release, almost like a trail... we might be able to lure them away. They'd follow the dark matter particles instead of focusing on us."

Shannon's eyes lit up with understanding. "Like tossing scraps of food to keep a pack of wolves at bay. That... could work."

Burke nodded, considering the idea. "It's risky. If we release too much, we'll drain our core, and we'll be left without enough power to get out of here. But if we don't try, we may not have a chance to escape at all."

He looked around the bridge, meeting the eyes of each member of his crew. This would be a gamble, and a dangerous one. But there was no other option.

"Alright, Connor," Burke said finally. "Get down to Engineering and set up a controlled dark matter release. Just enough to lure them away from us, but not enough to cripple the ship."

Connor nodded, his face tense with concentration. "I'm on it, Captain."

As Connor headed for the lift, Burke turned back to the viewscreen, watching the creatures drifting even closer. They were circling in tighter now, their hunger palpable in every movement.

"Shannon, prepare to follow Connor's trail as soon as it's laid out. Jones, monitor the creatures' positions. We need to be ready to move as soon as they take the bait."

His team sprang into action, each member focused and determined. Burke felt a swell of pride and responsibility as he watched them. They were all counting on him to get them through this. And somewhere, out there, Rebecca was waiting for him, wondering if he'd ever make it home.

Minutes ticked by like hours as they waited. Finally, Connor's voice crackled over the comm. "Captain, we're ready. Dark matter release in three... two... one."

On the viewscreen, a faint, sensor enhanced trail of particles began to drift away from the *Destiny*, like a breadcrumb path in the darkness. The creatures paused, their movements slowing as they seemed to sense the presence of dark matter.

"Come on... come on..." Burke whispered, holding his breath.

One by one, the creatures turned, drawn to the trail of particles. They drifted away from the *Destiny*, their massive forms following the dark matter like moths to a flame. The bridge crew watched in tense silence, each of them afraid to even breathe too loudly, as the creatures slowly moved away.

"Shannon, take us out," Burke ordered, his voice barely more than a whisper.

Shannon eased the ship forward, guiding the *Destiny* away from the creatures and back toward the path the buoy had laid out for them. Every second felt like an eternity, but finally, the creatures were behind them, their attention fixed on the trail of dark matter left in their wake.

As the *Destiny* pulled away from the void and back toward the edge of normal space, Burke allowed himself a sigh of relief.

They weren't safe yet, but they had escaped the immediate threat.

"Let's keep moving," he said, his voice low but resolute. "We've got a long way to go... but we're getting out of here."

Then suddenly the Rift flared with searing white light...a ship was coming through!

Chapter 9: Into the Rift

Rebecca Burke stood on the bridge of the *ESS Explorer*, her father's current pride and joy, and the most advanced starship ever built by Shepherd Industries—at least, it would be, once it was finished. Right now, it was a half-complete ship with barely-functional systems, an inexperienced crew, and a captain who was not meant to be here. But that didn't matter. What mattered was that she was here to find John.

The Rift loomed on the viewscreen, a swirling darkness alive with alien light. It looked like a massive, starless hole in the sky, surrounded by shifting colors that cast ghostly glows across the bridge. Rebecca knew that somewhere beyond that terrifying darkness, John was waiting. And she was going to bring him home.

"Approach vector confirmed, Captain," called Lieutenant Jiro Takeda, the young navigator whose experience was limited to simulators and a few short-range training flights. He was nervous, she could tell, but he had the steely resolve that most of the green crew shared. They were all doing their best, but this was no training mission.

"Thank you, Lieutenant," she said, trying to keep her voice steady to reassure the crew. Inside, she felt a knot of fear. She wasn't a military captain; she was an engineer. She'd overseen the

Explorer's design and construction, but that hardly prepared her to lead it on a rescue mission into unknown space.

The truth was, she'd taken a huge risk. The *Explorer* wasn't ready for this. The ship's main weapons—static torpedoes—hadn't even been installed yet. The launchers sat empty, waiting for next Tuesday's scheduled installation. The main engine core was only partially functional, with redundant systems still offline. They had a few tractor beams and minimal shields, and the auxiliary systems were patchy at best. They had just enough power to limp to the Rift, but any unexpected challenge could spell disaster.

She was beginning to wonder if she'd made a terrible mistake.

"Captain, gravitational readings are increasing," said Ensign Dara Nari, the young officer at the science console. She looked up with wide eyes. "The Rift... it's pulling us in!"

Rebecca's heart skipped a beat. She'd known the Rift had an intense gravitational field, but they were supposed to be well outside its reach. Clearly, the readings they'd relied on were wrong.

"Engage reverse thrusters! Full power!" she ordered, her voice sharp.

The bridge filled with the low hum of the thrusters, but the ship barely slowed. The pull of the Rift was overpowering, dragging them closer with a terrifying, relentless force. The *Explorer* shuddered under the strain, and warning lights flared across the control panels.

"Main engines!" Rebecca barked. "Give me everything we've got!"

The half-completed engine core roared to life, filling the ship with vibrations as it struggled to counter the pull of the Rift. But the force was too strong, and the ship continued to slip closer to the swirling darkness.

"It's not enough, Captain!" shouted Lieutenant Takeda, his voice edged with panic. "The engines aren't holding!"

Rebecca clenched her jaw, refusing to give in to the fear rising inside her. The Rift loomed closer on the viewscreen, an endless, churning vortex that seemed hungry, alive. It was nothing like anything she'd seen before—an unnatural tear in space that devoured everything in its path.

"Brace for impact!" she yelled. "All hands, brace yourselves!"

The *Explorer* shook violently as it crossed the event horizon. Gravity shifted, pulling them in every direction at once, and Rebecca gripped the armrests of her chair as the bridge lights flickered. The ship lurched, the partially functional systems struggling to cope with the strain. Sparks flew from several consoles, and she heard the frightened cries of her crew.

"Captain, shields are fluctuating! We're losing power in multiple sections!" shouted Commander Sasha Price, her usually calm demeanor fraying under the chaos.

Rebecca took a steadying breath. She couldn't let the crew see her panic. They were relying on her to stay strong, to lead them out of this mess. She had to focus on the one thing she knew: keeping the ship together, even if it meant patching systems on the fly.

"Reroute all auxiliary power to the shields," she ordered. "Cut life support in non-essential areas if you have to. Just keep us intact."

The bridge trembled, the hull groaning under the pressure. She knew that they had little to no defensive capability. Their torpedo launchers sat empty, the static torpedoes they did have sitting in storage with no way to launch them. They had a few tractor beams, but they were meant for cargo hauling, not for saving a ship from a cosmic nightmare.

"Structural integrity is at 60 percent and dropping, Captain!" called Nari.

Rebecca forced herself to think, to find a solution. "Can we use the tractor beams to anchor ourselves against the pull?"

Price looked doubtful but quickly tapped into her console. "It might slow us down. But there's nothing solid to latch onto out here. It'll only buy us a few seconds."

"Do it," Rebecca commanded. "Every second counts."

The tractor beams activated, latching onto the Rift's gravitational pull and creating a counterforce, but it was like trying to push back a tidal wave with bare hands. The ship slowed briefly, but the beams flickered, straining under the intensity.

The Rift dragged them deeper, and Rebecca could feel the *Explorer* slipping into a chaotic, distorted reality. The view outside was a kaleidoscope of colors and shapes, unnatural light twisting and stretching around them as they descended into the Rift's realm.

"Hold together," she murmured to herself, as if willing the ship to stay intact. "Come on, *Explorer*. Hold together."

Finally, with a shuddering lurch, the tractor beams overloaded, snapping back as the ship fell farther into the Rift. The bridge fell silent, except for the quiet hum of failing systems and the soft gasps of the crew. They were through. Or at least, they had crossed some threshold, because the pull had lessened, leaving them in a strange, silent place.

Rebecca exhaled shakily, her hands still clutching the armrests.

"Status report," she managed, her voice steadier than she felt.

Price surveyed the readouts, her face pale but focused. "Shields are at minimal strength. Hull integrity is... critical in some areas. Engines are holding, but auxiliary power is almost depleted. We're... stable, but just barely."

Rebecca looked around at her exhausted, rattled crew. They had survived. Somehow, this half-finished ship and its inexperienced team had made it through the Rift. But now they were adrift in a strange, dark region of space, cut off from everything they knew.

And somewhere, in this empty, alien void, was the *Destiny*—and her husband.

"Re-establish life support to all sections," Rebecca ordered. "Begin a full scan of the area. We're not going back until we find them."

The *Explorer* was battered and barely holding together, but Rebecca's resolve had only strengthened. She had come this far, and she wasn't leaving without John.

As the crew scrambled to recover, Rebecca looked out at the inky blackness, "some rescue ship!" she thought," hoping that she hadn't pushed it to far.

Chapter 10: Unexpected Entrance

The bridge of the *ESS Destiny* was buzzing with tension as Captain John Burke watched the glowing edges of the Rift. They had mapped an escape route out of the void, following the light that had guided them, and after what felt like a lifetime of survival in this nightmarish realm, they were finally on the verge of making their way home. The stars beyond the Rift were visible—faint but familiar, twinkling with the promise of safety, of Earth, of Rebecca.

"Captain, the engines are stable, and our course is plotted," reported Jones Mackenzie, the ship's navigator. Despite the fatigue etched on his face, he looked hopeful, even relieved. "We're ready to move on your command."

John nodded, the stars drawing him in like a lifeline. He took a deep breath, steeling himself. "Let's bring everyone home."

Just as he was about to give the order, a sudden, blinding flare erupted from the edges of the Rift, filling the bridge with an intense light. Burke shielded his eyes, his heart hammering as he tried to make sense of the surge. The Rift twisted and contorted, as if it were being torn open by some immense force.

"Captain! We're picking up another ship!" shouted Masters, his voice cutting through the chaos. His hands flew over the console as he tried to adjust the sensors, eyes wide with astonishment. "It's... it's the *Explorer*!"

Burke's breath caught in his throat. The *Explorer*. His mind reeled as he processed the impossible sight unfolding before him. He leaned forward, his eyes locked on the viewscreen as a battered, half-finished ship began to emerge from the blinding light of the Rift. The *Explorer* looked barely intact, its hull scarred, its thrusters flickering as it struggled to break free from the Rift's grip. Yet, there it was, an illusion of hope made real.

"Rebecca..." he whispered, a mixture of relief and fear twisting within him.

But their reunion was cut short. The ship-wide alarms screamed to life, and the lights dimmed to blood-red emergency status as a new threat loomed over them.

"Captain, we've got movement!" shouted Jones, his fingers flying across the control panel. His face was pale as he looked up, eyes wide. "It's the Voidless!"

The creatures had been lurking, stalking them in the depths of the void, their massive, shadowy forms almost invisible against the darkness. They were creatures born of the void, feeding on dark matter to sustain themselves, but the energy surge from the Rift's opening had drawn their attention like a flare. And now, they had two ships in their sights.

On the screen, Burke could see the alien shapes gathering at the edges of the Rift, their forms swirling and undulating, shadows with glimpses of teeth and tendrils that seemed to hunger for the ship's very essence. These creatures weren't just animals—they were predators of the void, and they were starving.

"We're sitting ducks out here!" Connor Vincente, the chief engineer, yelled, his voice tinged with desperation. "Our shields won't hold if they decide to attack!"

"Captain, the *Explorer* is signaling!" Shannon reported, her eyes locked on the display as the message came through.

"Patch them through!" Burke ordered, his voice resolute even as he tried to control his racing heart.

Rebecca's face appeared on the screen, framed by sparks and flickering lights. Her eyes were intense, her expression strained but determined. "John, we're here... but we're barely holding together," she said, voice crackling with static. "Our engine core is incomplete, and we've only got a handful of weapons that don't even have launch capabilities."

Burke's mind raced. The *Explorer* was in no state to defend itself, and neither ship had the power to face the creatures alone. If they didn't act fast, both ships would be ripped apart by the ravenous Voidless.

"Rebecca, listen," he said, gripping the edge of his console. "Those creatures are drawn to the Rift's energy. We have to move quickly and together to create a distraction—something that will let us slip away without them swarming us."

Rebecca nodded, her gaze fierce. "Our tractor beams aren't much, but we could use them to create a pulse... maybe scatter some debris to divert the creatures' attention."

"Perfect," Burke said, already forming a plan in his mind. "*Destiny* will handle the majority of the output. We'll create a pulse, draw the creatures to one side of the Rift, then both ships will make a break for the other side."

Rebecca gave him a grim smile. "Just like old times."

They shared a fleeting look, the distance and danger between them momentarily forgotten. But the next second, the reality of their situation crashed back down as another Voidless surged close to the *Destiny*, snapping its jaws in the direction of the ship.

"Connor, can we reroute any auxiliary power to reinforce the tractor beams?" Burke shouted.

Connor nodded, already working at his console. "It'll drain some of our other systems, but we'll make it happen, Captain."

"Do it. Shannon, coordinate with the *Explorer*. I want those tractor beams synchronized."

The two ships maneuvered into position, working as one to aim the beams at nearby fragments of torn apart space debris. It was risky—any miscalculation, and they could end up with debris damaging their own hulls. But it was the best chance they had to draw the creatures away.

"Tractor beams at full power!" Shannon announced.

The beams pulsed, grabbing hold of fragments of dark matter floating in the void. They intensified, creating a shimmering field that glowed brighter, casting an alluring target. The Voidless shifted, their attention momentarily captured as they began circling the light, drawn by the sudden surge of energy and movement.

"Now, break away!" Burke ordered.

Both ships veered off, engines struggling as they sped toward the opening in the void. Burke gritted his teeth, watching the creatures out of the corner of his eye as they continued to swarm around the light. For a moment, it seemed as if the plan was working—until one of the Voidless turned, its many eyes focusing on the fleeing ships.

"Captain, one of them is coming after us!" Jones yelled, panic flaring in his voice.

"Hold steady," Burke said, his voice steely. "Rebecca, we're going to need one more pulse."

Rebecca's voice came over the comm, tense but steady. "Understood. Ready on your mark."

"On three... two... one. Now!"

Another pulse burst from the *Explorer*'s tractor beams, more powerful than the last. The creature paused, torn between the ships and the enticing glow. With a lurch, it turned back toward the light, joining its brethren in the feeding frenzy around the debris.

"Now! All power to the engines!" Burke ordered.

Both ships accelerated, racing through the thinning edges of the Rift as the creatures swarmed around the false feast they had created. The stars grew brighter, sharper, as they finally broke free of the void, leaving the nightmare realm and its hungry inhabitants behind.

Silence fell on the *Destiny*'s bridge, a stunned, disbelieving quiet that resonated with the crew's shock and relief.

"We... we did it," whispered Jones, slumping back in his chair, visibly shaken but alive.

Burke let out a slow breath, looking at the stars beyond, feeling the tension draining from his shoulders. "Report status," he said, though his voice trembled.

Connor's voice came over the comm, exhausted but triumphant. "Hull integrity is holding. Minor damage to the outer decks, but nothing critical. We're... we're alive, Captain."

Burke's gaze shifted back to the screen, where the battered and crumpled *Explorer* held position nearby. He reached out, opening the comms link. "Rebecca," he said softly, his voice filled with relief. "We're safe."

Rebecca's face appeared, exhausted but smiling, and for the first time in what felt like an eternity, they both allowed themselves to breathe.

"We'll get you home," she said, her voice laced with determination and love. "Together."

"Not yet. I'm afraid we have some surgery to preform." Replied John with a tired smile.

Chapter 11: Out of the Shadows

The *ESS Destiny* and the *Explorer* floated together in open space, the stars clear and serene around them—a stunning contrast to the challenges they'd just survived. The crew on both ships was worn down to their core, many still reeling from the adrenaline-fueled flight out of the void. For a brief, blissful moment, silence reigned.

On the *Destiny*'s bridge, Captain John Burke let out a long breath, finally allowing himself a moment to absorb their success. They had made it. Against all odds they had escaped the void and survived its dark horrors. He glanced at the image of the *Explorer* on his monitor and felt a surge of pride—and relief.

But then, a sound broke through his reverie. It was a warning alarm, sharp and insistent.

"Captain!" Shannon O'Neil's voice was urgent as she scanned the monitors in disbelief. "I'm detecting an anomaly just outside the Rift."

Burke's stomach dropped. "What kind of anomaly?"

"It's…" Shannon's face paled as she stared at the readings. "One of the Voidless. It must have ridden our wake and breached the barrier with us."

The weight of her words sank in. They hadn't entirely escaped. One of the Voidless—those monstrous, predatory creatures—had followed them through. And now it was loose in real space.

"How!" Burke muttered, running a hand over his face as he turned to his crew. "If we don't contain it, that thing could devastate anything it comes across. It was created to feed on dark matter, to keep things in balance, but out here... who knows what it'll latch onto."

"We can't just leave it," Shannon said, a note of desperation in her voice. "We have to get it back into the void—or destroy it."

On the monitor, Burke could see the shadowy form of the creature, darker than the surrounding space, its jagged tendrils and shifting mass barely distinguishable. The creature seemed confused, disoriented, as if adjusting to the new environment, but it was quickly gaining cohesion, its tendrils stretching out like hungry feelers, sensing its new surroundings.

"We're going to need both ships to handle this," Burke said, his voice hardening with determination. He opened a comm line to the *Explorer*. "Rebecca, are you reading this?"

Rebecca's voice crackled over the comm, filled with a mix of grim determination and exhaustion. "Loud and clear, John. We see it. But the *Explorer* isn't fully operational yet—we barely have weapons, and the engine core is incomplete."

Burke clenched his jaw, thinking. The *Explorer* didn't have any fully operational weapons, but it did have a few static torpedoes. While these torpedoes weren't designed to launch, they could still be used if they found a way to place them close enough to the creature.

"We'll have to make do," Burke replied. "The *Destiny* will try to get the creature's attention. If we can lure it away from the

Rift, we might be able to knock it off balance with the static torpedoes. It'll be risky, but if we can push it back toward the Rift, we might have a chance to throw it back through."

Rebecca hesitated but then nodded. "Understood. We'll set up a tractor beam to guide a few torpedoes. If you can distract it, we can try to detonate the torpedoes near it and force it back."

"Let's get to work," Burke said, a steely resolve settling over him. "We're not letting this thing roam free."

He closed the comm and turned to his crew. "Alright, team. Shannon, I want you to keep a lock on that creature's position. Jones, plot a course that keeps us just outside its reach but close enough to draw its attention."

Both officers nodded, their expressions tense but focused. As the *Destiny* closed in on the creature, Burke watched as it seemed to recognize their presence. The creature shifted, tendrils unfurling, sensing the ship as if tasting the air, drawn to the faint energy traces radiating from the *Destiny*'s engines.

"It's responding to us, Captain," Shannon reported. "It's... it's definitely responding!."

"Good," Burke said, though his nerves were frayed. "Keep us moving—don't let it get too close."

On the monitor, he could see the *Explorer* maneuvering nearby, its tractor beam pulling a few static torpedoes slowly toward the creature. Without proper launchers, they had to rely on the tractor beam to place the torpedoes in close proximity, a slow and delicate process.

"Rebecca," Burke called over the comm. "We're ready on our end. Position those torpedoes as close as you can without endangering your ship."

"Understood," Rebecca's voice came back, tense but steady. "We're bringing them in. Just... keep that thing's attention."

Burke grimaced as he watched the creature lurch forward, its tendrils stretching out toward the *Destiny*. Its hunger seemed to intensify, drawn to the unfamiliar energy it detected.

"Shields holding, but it's starting to drain power," Connor Vincente reported, his voice tight. "We're not going to last if it gets any closer."

"Hold steady," Burke ordered, his gaze locked on the screen as the *Explorer* continued to position the torpedoes. "Just a little longer..."

The creature closed in, its dark mass casting an unnatural shadow over the *Destiny*. Burke could almost feel its presence, an oppressive weight pressing down on the ship.

Then, a spark of light caught his eye on the monitor. The torpedoes were finally in position, suspended just beyond the creature's reach.

"Rebecca, now!" Burke shouted.

The *Explorer*'s crew detonated the static torpedoes, releasing an intense burst of energy that cascaded across the creature's form. The Voidless recoiled, its tendrils flaring in pain as it writhed in the blast. The shockwave of energy caused it to lose cohesion, its form temporarily destabilizing and flickering.

"Now's our chance! All engines, full thrust—push it back toward the Rift!" Burke ordered, his voice rising with urgency.

Both the *Destiny* and the *Explorer* powered up their engines, creating a surge of force that pressed against the creature, driving it backward. The Voidless struggled, its tendrils thrashing wildly as it tried to resist, but the coordinated force of both ships kept it moving, inch by inch, back toward the Rift's threshold.

"We're almost there!" Shannon shouted, her voice filled with hope.

As they neared the Rift's edge, the creature seemed to sense what was happening. It convulsed, one final thrash as it tried to break free, but the combined energy from both ships was too strong. With one final pulse, the Rift itself seemed to pull the creature back, dragging it throuh the shimmering barrier and back into the darkness.

The Rift pulsed once, then stilled. The creature was gone, swallowed back into the void from which it came.

A tense silence filled the bridge as the crew collectively exhaled, the reality of their success sinking in. Burke slumped back in his chair, the weight of the ordeal finally lifting.

"We did it," he murmured, barely able to believe it.

On the view screen, Rebecca's face appeared, exhausted but smiling. "Nice work, Captain Burke."

He grinned, relief flooding through him. "Couldn't have done it without you, Captain Burke."

The comm line was quiet for a moment as they both took in the vast, peaceful expanse of space around them. After everything they'd been through, they were finally free. Together.

"Now how do we seal this tear in space?," Rebecca said softly, her voice filled with warmth.

Chapter 12: Closing the Rift

The *ESS Destiny* and the *ESS Explorer* floated in a precarious calm just outside the Rift. The crew had barely recovered from their ordeal in the void, and the battered hulls of both ships bore testament to the struggle they'd faced. But Captain John Burke knew that they couldn't rest just yet. The Rift, still open, was a looming threat to the entire sector, and they were the only ones with the chance to close it.

"Captain, I'm still picking up traces of that light beacon," Shannon O'Neil, the *Destiny*'s pilot, said, her eyes glued to her console. "It's faint, but the signature's still there—like it's embedded within the Rift itself."

John nodded, still perplexed by the mystery of the beacon. "It was leading us. Protecting us from the creatures. But... who or what could have created something so advanced? And why would they want to help us?"

There was silence on the bridge as everyone pondered this question. The beacon had saved them, guiding them back to familiar stars, but its purpose and origin remained unknown.

Grant Masters, the operations officer, turned toward Burke, his expression pensive. "Captain, whoever created that beacon seemed to know about the Rift and the dangers it held. If we're ever going to solve this mystery, we'll need to make sure the Rift is contained for good."

Burke nodded. "And to do that, we'll need to seal it. We can't leave it open like this; it's too dangerous."

Connor Vincente, the *Destiny*'s chief engineer, cleared his throat. "I think I might have a solution, Captain. It's risky, but it could work."

"Go ahead, Connor," Burke said, hopeful.

Connor's eyes gleamed with an idea. "If we treat the Rift like a wound, we could attempt to 'stitch' it closed. We could use our static torpedoes as conductive nodes to create an electromagnetic field across the Rift, essentially pulling its edges together and forcing it to seal."

"Like a suture," Rebecca Burke's voice came over the comm from the *Explorer*. "But it would take a lot of precision to get the torpedoes in exactly the right positions on each side of the Rift. One mistake, and the field might destabilize."

Burke turned to Jones Mackenzie, his navigator and longtime friend. "Jones, think you can get us close enough to deploy torpedoes on our side of the Rift while maintaining a safe distance?"

Jones gave a tight smile. "Close calls are what I live for, Captain. I'll get us where we need to be. But we'll need Rebecca's team on the *Explorer* to do the same on their end."

Rebecca's voice was calm but determined. "Understood, John. We'll need to coordinate each torpedo placement exactly."

Connor set to work with his team, configuring the static torpedoes to emit an electromagnetic pulse when triggered. Normally, the torpedoes were built for non-lethal containment and subduing targets, but with some modifications, they could function as powerful nodes to create the field across the Rift.

The *Destiny* and *Explorer* moved into their respective positions, each ship carefully maneuvering along the sides of the Rift, maintaining just enough distance to avoid the powerful gravitational pull but staying close enough for precision deployment. Burke felt the tension across the bridge as they moved into position—one misstep, one wrong calculation, and they could get pulled back into the void.

"Deploying first torpedo," Shannon announced as she guided the *Destiny* in, steady hands on the controls. The torpedo slid out from the *Destiny*'s bay, drifting into the Rift's gravitational boundary. It hung there for a moment, caught in the delicate pull of space, before Connor adjusted its trajectory with a subtle adjustment from the ship's guidance systems.

"First torpedo in place," Connor reported, wiping the sweat from his brow. "We need five more along this side to create a stable field."

Rebecca's voice crackled through the comm. "*Explorer* deploying first torpedo now."

On the *Explorer*, Rebecca watched with bated breath as her crew, inexperienced and working with an unfinished ship, navigated the tense deployment. They were relying on makeshift guidance controls and a partially powered engine core to hold their position. But her crew was determined, focused, and they managed to set the first torpedo on the opposite side of the Rift.

With each torpedo placement, the edges of the Rift seemed to respond, flickering faintly as if aware of the forces moving around it. As they continued the deployment, the electromagnetic field began to take shape, a faint, glowing lattice forming between the torpedoes. It was like an invisible thread sewing the Rift's dark edges together.

"Final torpedo on the *Destiny* side is in place," Connor reported, his voice barely hiding his relief. "We're holding stable."

"*Explorer* has the last torpedo ready," Rebecca said. "Initiating deployment... now."

The final torpedo slid into its designated position, completing the circuit. Burke watched as the two rows of torpedoes formed a shimmering outline along the Rift's jagged edges. The faint glow of the electromagnetic field began to intensify as the energy built up between them, pulling at the Rift's edges, encouraging them to draw together.

"Connor, initiate the current," Burke ordered, his voice steady but tense.

Connor activated the field, and a hum filled the bridge as power surged from the *Destiny*'s core into the line of torpedoes. The torpedoes flared to life, glowing brighter as they pushed an electromagnetic current across the Rift. The *Explorer* did the same, sending its energy into the connected nodes.

The Rift began to react, its edges warping and pulling inward, resisting the force that tried to close it. The dark, jagged line shivered and twisted, as if trying to keep itself open, but the current held firm, keeping the Rift's edges locked in place.

"It's working," Shannon whispered, her eyes wide with awe.

The Rift continued to close, its edges inching toward one another, pulled by the field. But then, suddenly, it buckled, sending a shockwave through space that rattled both ships.

"Hold steady!" Burke shouted. "Increase the current if needed!"

Connor adjusted the power flow, pushing the limits of the *Destiny*'s engine core. The field intensified, and the Rift began to collapse faster, as if it were finally succumbing to the force.

On the *Explorer*, Rebecca worked with her engineering team, pushing the ship's unfinished systems to their limits. Her crew was tired, anxious, and undertrained, but their resolve held firm. They kept the current stable, holding the Rift in place as its edges drew closer.

With a final, agonizing pulse, the edges of the Rift touched, merging together. For a moment, it looked as if the tear might reopen, fighting against the closure. But the combined electromagnetic fields locked it in place, and with a soft, almost anticlimactic implosion, the Rift vanished, leaving only empty space and drained torpedoes in it's wake.

Cheers erupted on both bridges as the crew of the *Destiny* and *Explorer* celebrated, relief washing over them. They had done it. The Rift was closed, the void sealed away.

Burke let out a long breath, his shoulders finally relaxing as he looked around at his exhausted but triumphant crew. "Grant, collect those spent torpedoes and lets get home." –"I Sir" Masters replied.

"Good work, everyone," Burke said, pride evident in his voice. He opened the comm link to the *Explorer*. "Rebecca, you and your crew did an incredible job."

Rebecca's voice came back, warm and steady. "We all did, John. It was... touch and go there for a bit, but we made it."

As the two ships drifted together in the quiet aftermath, Burke's mind returned to the question that lingered in the background—the beacon that had guided them, the mysterious force that had saved them. Whoever had placed it in the Rift had known they would need help, and they had provided it without asking anything in return.

"We may never know who—or what—placed that beacon," he murmured, almost to himself. "But whoever they are... we owe them our lives."

As the *Destiny* and *Explorer* set a course for home, the question of the beacon's origins stayed with Burke. The Rift was closed, but he knew that this encounter was only the beginning of a much larger mystery. They would simply have to wait for the next chapter to unfold.

Chapter 13: The Source of the Light

John Burke leaned back in his chair on the *ESS Destiny's* bridge, staring at the faint blue glow of the Rift as it continued to stabilize, the last remnants of their work sealing it away from the universe. It was a patchwork job, using the static torpedoes to "stitch" the Rift together with bursts of energy, like a thread woven across the wound in space. They had managed to contain it—for now.

But John's mind was still elsewhere, troubled by the memory of the beacon, the light that had led them out of the void when all hope had been lost. That light, somehow, had felt... familiar. A presence, almost, reaching through the Rift to guide them home. And in the deepest part of his mind, John couldn't shake the feeling that he'd heard a voice, faint and distant, something comforting yet indescribably sad.

Who—or what—had saved them?

Rebecca sat nearby, a silent strength in her gaze as she glanced out the viewport. She had risked everything to find him, even taking the half-finished *Explorer* into the Rift's deadly pull. He could feel the questions lingering between them, ones neither had spoken aloud since their narrow escape.

Finally, Rebecca broke the silence. "John, I know you felt it too. I reviewed the data log. That light wasn't just... energy. It was something. Someone."

John hesitated, glancing at her. Rebecca's eyes, so often filled with determination, now held a hint of fear, the same fear that clawed at his heart. "Yes," he said slowly, "it was like a memory just out of reach. But familiar, like... someone I knew."

They sat in silence, the hum of the ship's systems the only sound around them. John's mind was far away, sifting through old memories, voices, echoes of the past.

And then, it came to him—fragmented, like broken pieces of a dream. His father. Long gone now, but the memory was sharp and piercing. His father had been a captain too, decades ago, on one of the early NASA exploratory missions before the age of Tachyon drives. He'd disappeared on a mission when John was still a child, his ship was never recovered, lost somewhere beyond the far reaches of known space.

"Do you think it could be...?" Rebecca whispered, as if reading his thoughts.

John clenched his jaw. It seemed impossible. His father's ship had vanished decades before. The entire mission had been classified and buried by NASA, a story so old it had become almost myth. But the voice, the presence—he couldn't ignore the feeling that it had been him, guiding them out.

Exercising some computer skills he almost forgot he had John accessed the mission logs, pulling up the encrypted records from the old files. If there was any trace of communication embedded within the beacon's transmission, any hint of a signature, they'd find it there. Finally, the console pinged. Eyes widened as they read the data.

"It's a message," Rebecca breathed. "But not just any message... It's from a NASA prototype ship from decades ago.

The *Star Bright*." Her voice trembled slightly, a mix of fear and awe. "This is amazing!"

It says "The Star Bright mission went missing on a test flight beyond the far edges of explored space, decades ago. Everyone assumed it was destroyed. But..."She gestured to the data, and John saw it—embedded in the beacon's signal was a complex pattern, a sequence that pulsed and repeated like a heartbeat. It was faint, degraded by time and distance, but unmistakable. An encoded warning call, repeated endlessly, reaching out into the void.

"But why would he be out here?" John asked, a deep frown creasing his brow. "If the ship vanished decades ago, how is he even—"

"John," Rebecca interrupted softly, "what if he never died? What if he became... something else?"

They looked at each other, the weight of her words settling over them. The idea was absurd, yet there it was—the possibility that somewhere, trapped on the other side of the Rift, his father's consciousness had survived, transformed into a beacon, an echo of the man he'd once been. The *Star Bright* had never returned because it had been pulled into the void, its crew lost to the darkness. And somehow, his father had found a way to reach back, to call out across the Rift.

But how?

As they continued analyzing the data, a theory began to take shape—a theory as wild as it was disturbing. The *Star Bright's* original drive had been experimental, dangerous. It wasn't just a ship lost to the void; it was a key. It must have created a Rift itself, an unintended consequence of a drive malfunction. His father, had accidentally ripped a hole in space, condemning himself and his crew to an eternity of darkness. But not before he and his crew built a warning buoy. Encoding it with a human/ai interface. this "light" beacon would interface with any ship and warn them off.

And now, seeing that another ship had been drawn into another rift, it had reached out to warn them, to pull them away before they could fall victim to the same fate.

"He saved us," John murmured, awe and sorrow mixing in his voice. "After all these years..."

John closed his eyes, grappling with the enormity of it. They'd sealed the Rift, patched it together with the torpedoes—but if they ever opened it again, if they dared reach into that darkness, they might find his father, or what remained of him and his ship, trapped in that void.

"We'll find a way to honor him," John said, placing a comforting hand on Rebecca's shoulder. "But for now, we have to focus on what's ahead. There's still so much we don't understand about the Rift, about the consequences of what we've done. The universe might not be ready to face what's on the other side."

Rebeecca nodded, wiping her tears. "You're right."

They sat in silence for a moment, both absorbing the weight of what they'd discovered. And though they had escaped, they both knew that some part of the Rift's mystery would forever be entwined with their own lives, a reminder that humanity's reach often exceeded its grasp.

As they prepared to send their final reports back to Shepherd Industries, John knew this mission would be remembered not only as an exploration of the unknown, but as a warning—a reminder of the cost of mistakes, and the sacrifices that lay hidden in the depths of space. And though this Rift had closed, he couldn't shake the feeling that one day, another would call to them again.

Epilogue: Micah Shepherd's Perspective

Micah Shepherd stood in his office, high above the glistening expanse of New Boston, watching the sunset paint the city skyline in deep hues of orange and violet. The light refracted off the ocean far below, creating a shimmering mirror effect that stretched across the waves. He found himself staring into that distant horizon, searching it as if it might hold answers he desperately wanted but feared.

The *ESS Destiny* and *ESS Explorer* had returned days ago, emerging from the stars as battered, weary heroes. It was time to rebuild and improve. The news had swept through every media outlet, hailing the crews as pioneers, survivors of the uncharted realms beyond the Rift. The stories painted the mission as a great triumph for Shepherd Industries and humankind's exploration of deep space. But Micah knew that the reality was far more complex.

He had heard firsthand from Rebecca, the details of what they'd encountered—the void, the creatures, and the Rift's cataclysmic forces. She had spoken about the beacon, a mysterious light that had guided them when all hope seemed lost, and of John's unyielding determination, his sheer will to protect his crew even when it had seemed that all was lost.

John Burke, Micah thought, his lips tightening. He felt torn. He was proud beyond words of his daughter's bravery, her resourcefulness in the face of danger. But he couldn't shake the pang of guilt. He had known the risks of pushing the Explorer's schedule forward, of letting Rebecca launch before it was fully operational. But she had insisted, desperate to find John, and Micah hadn't been able to deny her. Now that she was safe, he questioned himself—was it fatherly support, or weakness that had let him relent? The line had blurred in the heat of the moment.

He picked up the report again, flipping through its pages as if searching for something hidden between the lines. Rebecca's account and John's mission logs painted a picture of survival, resilience, and ingenuity. But what truly concerned Micah was the Rift itself, that inexplicable scar in the fabric of reality—a wound born from Tachyon technology, his technology.

Micah's eyes drifted to a small, polished frame on his desk. Inside it, an old photograph of Rebecca as a child, her eyes wide with wonder, gazing at the stars. She had always dreamed of exploration, always yearned to know what lay beyond the boundaries. He had supported her every step of the way, driven not only by his love for his daughter but also by his own desire to push humanity's limits, to leave a legacy that would endure beyond the constraints of time.

But now? Now, he felt the weight of that ambition, its shadows mixing with his pride. What had they unlocked out there? And at what cost? There had been something profoundly unsettling about the Rift, about the Voidless creatures that had nearly devoured his daughter, even though they were acting on instinct -they were hungry. A hunger caused by their intrusion.

The Rift's closure was supposed to be a victory, but Micah's instincts told him it was only the beginning of something much larger—and perhaps more dangerous—than any of them could understand.

"Sir?" A voice broke his reverie. It was his assistant, standing at the doorway, her voice laced with hesitation. "They're ready for you in the briefing room. The board wants an update on the next phase of the Tachyon Initiative."

Micah sighed, nodding. The board saw only the promise of profit, the power that tachyon technology could bring. They were eager to capitalize on this so-called victory, to launch further into the unknown. They didn't understand the risks, the unknown variables that still troubled him. He couldn't tell them about the beacon, couldn't explain that they had been saved not by their own ingenuity, but by something still unknown —waiting on the other side of the Rift.

"Tell them I'll be there shortly," he replied, dismissing his assistant with a wave of his hand.

As the door closed, Micah turned back to the window, his gaze fixed on the stars that were beginning to appear in the darkening sky. There was something out there, he knew it. Was it friend or foe? A guardian or a threat?

He placed the mission report down and ran a hand over his face, feeling the weight of years pressing down on him. There were days when he felt like he'd spent his entire life standing at the edge of an abyss, daring humanity to leap forward. But now, for the first time, he wondered if he'd gone too far.

The Rift was closed, but Micah knew that a door, once opened, could leave a scar. The laws of physics, of reality itself, had been tested. And scars had a way of reopening, especially when they were left untreated, unsolved. He knew his daughter and John would want answers, just as he did. But the answers might lead them back to the brink.

In his heart, Micah resolved to protect them, whatever the cost. He would continue his research, probe the unknown, and he would do it in a way that ensured no harm would come to Rebecca or John. He would shield them from whatever lay beyond, beyond comprehension. If he could.

Micah took a deep breath and turned away from the window, straightening his jacket. He had a legacy to safeguard, a family to protect. And while he couldn't silence the whispers of curiosity that gnawed at him, he knew he would face them on his terms.

Steeling himself, he walked toward the door, ready to address the board, to assure them of the Tachyon Initiative's "success." But deep within, he knew he would remain vigilant, watching for signs, waiting for a day when the unknown might reach out to them once more. When something special might be needed to save the day. What he did not know...yet.

As he stepped out of his office, a final thought crossed his mind -Next time, they might not have a beacon to guide them home.

Glossary of Terms:

1. **Tachyon Drive**
   - A hypothetical faster-than-light propulsion system that harnesses tachyons—particles that theoretically travel faster than light. In the story, tachyon drives are responsible for creating the Rift when improperly handled, as they manipulate space for interstellar travel.

2. **Rift**
   - A tear in the fabric of space-time caused by the collision of two ships' tachyon drives and antimatter engines. The Rift is a shimmering, unstable void that defies conventional physics and poses dangers to navigation and reality itself.

3. **Antimatter Engine**
   - A highly advanced propulsion system that uses antimatter and matter annihilation to produce immense energy. The collision of antimatter engines with tachyon drives created the Rift.

4. **Void**
   - A empty region beyond known space, accessible through the Rift. The Void contains alien creatures (the Voidless) and unique physics, making survival difficult for ships and humans.

5. **Voidless**
   - Large, predatory creatures that inhabit the Void. These entities feed on dark matter and were disturbed when the Rift upset the balance of dark matter in the region. They are highly dangerous and capable of breaching the Rift to enter normal space.

6. **Static Torpedoes**
   - Unarmed projectiles used for delivering electric charges or conducting experiments, such as sealing the Rift in the story. They are designed to create an electrical current.

7. **Dark Matter**
   - A theoretical form of matter that does not emit light or energy, making it invisible to traditional sensors. Dark matter is essential to the balance of the universe and serves as the food source for the Voidless creatures.

8. **Energy Stitching**
   - A technique used to stabilize and repair tears in space by creating a current across the Rift with static torpedoes. This process "sews" the fabric of space-time back together, though it is a temporary and experimental solution.

9. **Beacon**
   - A device or signal emitting light and data to guide ships through dangerous or unknown areas. In the story, the beacon is revealed to be an encoded signal from a long-lost ship, acting as both a warning and a guide.

10. **Gravitational Wake**
    - The disturbance or ripple in space caused by the movement of massive objects or ships, particularly those with advanced propulsion systems. The Voidless creature used the gravitational wake of the *Destiny* and *Explorer* to breach the Rift.

11. **Shepherd Industries**
    - The corporation responsible for building advanced starships like the *ESS Destiny* and *ESS Explorer*.

Known for its innovation, Shepherd Industries plays a critical role in humanity's exploration of space and the development of tachyon drive technology.

12. **Rift Stabilization**

    ◦ A process of using energy and advanced technology to prevent a Rift from growing or collapsing. In the story, this is achieved with makeshift methods, such as using static torpedoes and conducting energy currents.

13. **Parallel Dimension**

    ◦ An alternate universe or reality existing alongside the known universe. The Void is considered a parallel dimension, where laws of physics differ dramatically from those in our own.

14. **Quantum Entanglement**

    ◦ A phenomenon where particles become interconnected, so the state of one particle instantaneously affects the state of another, regardless of distance. While not directly explained in the story, this concept could underpin the tachyon communication systems and the beacon's ability to transmit messages
    ◦ through the Rift.

1. **Energy Surge**

    ◦ A sudden, immense burst of energy that can disrupt systems or structures. In the story, an energy surge from the Rift allows the *Explorer* to enter but also draws the attention of the Voidless creatures.

2. **Dimensional Breach**

    ◦ The act of crossing from one dimension to another, as

the *Explorer* and Voidless creature do when they are pulled into or escape from the Void through the Rift.

3. **Tachyon Signal Encoding**
   - A method of embedding information into tachyon-based transmissions. This is used by the beacon to send a repeating distress signal across dimensions, helping the *Destiny* escape the Void.

4. **Experimental Starship**
   - A prototype vessel equipped with untested or cutting-edge technology. Both the *Destiny* and the *Explorer* are experimental starships, pushing the limits of current science and technology.

5. **Rift Barrier**
   - The boundary between the Void and normal space, created by the instability of the Rift. The barrier must be sealed to prevent further incursions by the Voidless or other dangers.

1. **Interdimensional Physics**
   - A branch of theoretical physics that studies the interactions and properties of dimensions beyond the observable universe. This field underpins much of the technology and phenomena encountered in the story, including the Rift, Void, and tachyon drives.

This glossary provides a comprehensive reference to the scientific terms and concepts explored in *Crossing the Void*, helping readers navigate the technical and speculative elements of the story.

Don't miss out!

Visit the website below and you can sign up to receive emails whenever Grayson Gray publishes a new book. There's no charge and no obligation.

https://books2read.com/r/B-A-ONFXC-KMIJF

BOOKS 2 READ

Connecting independent readers to independent writers.

Also by Grayson Gray

Light Speed
Light Speed -Crossing Into the Void